Also by
JANICE MAY UDRY
A Tree is Nice

JANICE MAY UDRY

EMILY'S AUTUMN

Illustratrated by
Erik Blegvad

A WORLD'S WORK CHILDREN'S BOOK

Text © 1969 by Janice May Udry
Illustrations © 1969 by Erik Blegvad
All rights reserved
First published in Great Britain 1976 by
World's Work Ltd
The Windmill Press
Kingswood Tadworth Surrey

Printed in Great Britain by
Morrison and Gibb Ltd, London and Edinburgh

SBN 437 82181 1

EMILY'S AUTUMN

Do you know who made you, little cornhusk doll?

My own grandmother made you for me. You're just the kind of doll she had when she was a little girl a long time ago.

Now wrap up, dear. We're going out. It's cold today. We must shut the door.

This is my Grandmother's farm. If
I stand on this gate I can see the
barn, the fields, the woods, and even
the bridge over the stream.

Grandmother is in the kitchen
finishing the jam. Do you see her in the
window?

This morning we made bramble
jelly together. We'll have new jelly on
toast for supper tonight.

Now I am old enough to visit
Grandmother alone. When I was a
baby my sister Sarah used to come.
Edward, the baby, can't come by
himself yet.

When I'm the only one here
Grandmother has time to show me
how to sew and how they used to blow
bubbles with cotton reels.

Now she has time to tell me stories
about when Mother was a little girl.

All the others have gone back to
school. Sarah and my cousins are
gone now because summer is over.

Where did summer go, little cornhusk doll? Here by the gate are the last
of Grandmother's marigolds. They're
a little patch of summer, left over.

Would you like to have a name,
little cornhusk doll? Your name will
be Marigold. My name is Emily. Don't
forget.

What was summer? Roses were in bloom then. Pink and yellow roses were on the gate when we came.

The roses have names. Grandmother says one of them is called New Dawn. One is called Penelope and one is the Mermaid rose.

It must be fun to name roses and babies. Sarah chose Edward's name.

On all the hot days of summer, doors and windows were open. The bees, the butterflies, and my cousins went in and out, in and out.

We filled three mugs with runner bean seeds and put them on the front porch rail. We made hollyhock dolls and put them along the porch rail, too.

Edward was really little then. He took his nap in his pram in the shade.

We walked through the cornfield when it was green above my head, and Sarah sang, "Oh, never tell a secret in a cornfield 'cause the corn's got ears!"

In the evenings we went out to
answer the owls. They called
"Ooo-oo," from the woods.

Sarah and the others answered
blowing through cupped hands. I've
almost learned to do it, too.

We sat on one of Grandmother's
old quilts in the garden at night while
we looked at the stars.

On August Bank Holiday, a storm
came. We had to run back with
the baskets and have the picnic on
Grandmother's porch. But there was
a rainbow after the storm when we
were having the cake.

One day we drove all day to get to
the ocean The water was cool. The
sand was like brown sugar.

The sound of the ocean came in through
the little windows of the old beach house
on stilts while we were falling asleep.

In the morning we found shells and took them home in paper bags and buckets.

We made a seashell garden for Grandmother by her gate.

Then the fair came with a merry-go-round. And all the pigs and cows and rabbits at the fair won prizes.

There was a building with beautiful quilts on the walls and old-fashioned dolls.

We saw the lights of the fair at night. And we ate candyfloss going home.

That was summer when the roses were blooming over the gate and my cousins came.

That was summer when the woods were dark and deep.

That was when the kitten grew into a little cat.

And that was when we planted the seeds that grew all sorts of gourds and sunflowers that seemed to reach the sky.

Now listen, little cornhusk doll.
Those sounds in the woods are the
acorns falling. I even hear them in the
night.

Do you see the squirrels? They're
hurrying everywhere, up and down
the trees, hiding nuts in secret places.

Listen to the wind. It's a lullaby. Do you hear the trees sighing? Soon they will sleep.

Now I'll make a little leaf house for you, my cornhusk doll. A little house for you all made of bright yellow leaves. I'll make it here beside this log.

Here's a frog come to visit you.

Now I'll take you down to the old
bridge. Do you see the leaves floating
away like a million little boats?

Good-bye, leaves, good-bye.

"You may pick the last marigolds,
Emily. It's going to freeze tonight,"
Grandmother told me.

Wrap up well, little cornhusk doll, little Marigold.

Sing a lullaby to the trees. Say good-bye to the swallows. They're going to fly away for a while.

Shall we go in? The kitchen is warm and smells like jam.

We'll put the marigolds on the windowsill where Grandmother's cat sits looking out.